Library of Congress Cataloging-in-Publication Data
Bateman, Teresa.
A plump and perky turkey / by Teresa Bateman; illustrated by Jeff Shelly.
First Edition
p.   cm.
Summary: The townspeople of Squawk Valley try to trick a turkey into being their Thanksgiving dinner,
but are frustrated when the turkey tricks them instead.
ISBN: 1-890817-91-0
[1. Turkeys—fiction. 2. Stories in thyme.]
I. Shelly, Jeff, ill. II. Title.
PZ8.3.B314 Pl 2001
[E]—dc21   00-068535

Creative Director: Bretton Clark
Designed by: Billy Kelly
Editor: Francesca Crispino
The illustrations in this book were prepared with watercolor and gouache.
Printed in Belgium
First edition, 09/01
2 4 6 8 10 9 7 5 3 1

WINSLOW PRESS

Home Office: All inquiries:
770 East Atlantic Ave.   115 East 23rd Street
Suite 201   10th Floor
Delray Beach, FL 33483   New York, NY 10010

Discover *A Plump and Perky Turkey*'s interactive Web site with worldwide links, games, activities, and more at:

winslowpress.com

A Plump and Perky Turkey

To David, Paul, Kirk, Jake, Kris, Sam, and Joey, who would never, ever be fooled by a
clever turkey (even if the turkey were disguised as their aunt!)
T. B.

To my wife, Christine
J. S.

A Plump and Perky Turkey

By Teresa Bateman

Illustrated by Jeff Shelly

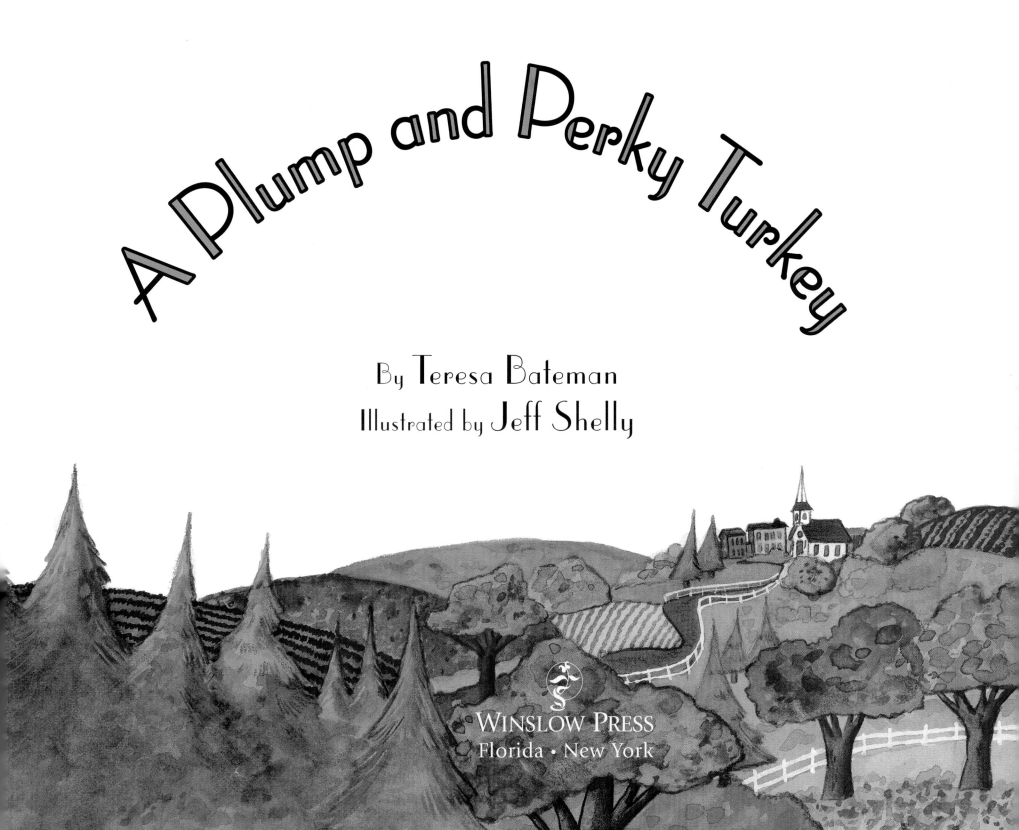

WINSLOW PRESS

Florida • New York

SQUAWK VALLEY
POST OFFICE

Fresh
SHREDDED
WHEAT

SQUAWK VALLEY
PRESS
TURKEYS
GONE!!

The people in Squawk Valley
   were downhearted and depressed.
Thanksgiving was approaching,
   but without its special guest.
They couldn't find a turkey
   for the feast they planned to eat.
It looked like they'd be making do
   with bowls of shredded wheat.

"A plump and perky turkey's
	what we need," they all agreed.
"But finding turkeys nowadays
	is very hard indeed.
The birds have gotten smarter,
	and they all seem quite aware
that it's best to disappear
	when autumn leaves are in the air."
A plump and perky turkey—
	stomachs rumbled at the thought.
But how to trick a turkey
	into jumping in the pot?

Then Ebenezer Beezer
    had a thought pop in his head.
"If we can't find a turkey,
    let's have one find us, instead!
We could hold an arts-and-crafts fair,"
    he declared, with wink and grin.
"A fair with one grand turkey prize—
    that *all* of us could win!

And since our goal is turkey,
   that's the theme we'll take to heart.
We'll fill our fair with folks and fun
   and tons of turkey art.

We'll make turkeys out of spuds

and out of clay and out of rope.

We'll make turkeys out of oatmeal,

out of paper, out of soap!

We'll hang a bunch of posters
     in the forest way down low,
to invite some turkey candidates
     to model for our show.
Why, even turkeys understand
     (as everybody knows)
you can't make turkey art
     without a turkey there to pose."

The people in Squawk Valley
held a poster jamboree!
They plastered their creations
onto every single tree.

Now it happened in Squawk Valley,
  lived a turkey known as Pete.
He was cocky, he was clever,
  and he really liked to eat.
While he strutted through the forest,
  plump and perky through the pines,
he was startled, and intrigued,
  by all those interesting signs.
With a proud and jaunty gobble,
  he gave out a hearty cry—
"A plump and perky turkey?
  Well, I'm sure I qualify."

Pete applied for the position,
   and he strutted plump and proud.
He could hardly wait to model
   for the large and eager crowd.
"Yer hired!" shouted Beezer,
   for the folks had all agreed
that Pete the Perky Turkey
   was the answer to their need.

'Twas the week before Thanksgiving
when Pete posed to do his part,
and the artsy-craftsy townsfolk
started making turkey art.

They made turkeys out of spuds

and out of clay and out of rope.

They made turkeys out of oatmeal,

out of paper, out of soap.

Thanksgiving Day, the artwork done,
    they asked the model down,
to judge their homemade turkeys
    and to pick the best in town.
"Now when the judging's over,"
    Beezer whispered with a smile,
"we'll tuck that model turkey
    in the oven for a while."

Pete judged each piece of artwork
as the hungry crowd all cheered.
He stopped to take a closer look,
and then . . . he disappeared!

There were turkeys made of spuds,
    there were turkeys made of rope.
There were turkeys made of paper,
    there were turkeys made of soap.
The room was full of turkeys,
    in a wall-to-wall collage.
For a clever bird like Pete
    it was a perfect camouflage.

"He's over here!" Old Beezer said.

"He's here!" said Jacob Green.

They searched amongst the turkeys,
but their bird had fled the scene.

A note in turkey scrawl they found,
half-hidden on the lawn:
"Good-bye. I took my modeling fee."
(The oatmeal bird was gone.)

The people in Squawk Valley
were left feeling rather blue.
The only turkeys left in town
appeared too hard to chew.
"Oh well," said Beezer brightly,
as they gathered 'round to eat.
"Right now, at least I'm thankful
that we still have shredded wheat."

That day folks learned a lesson
that stuck firm with them forever.
A plump and perky turkey
can be pretty doggone clever.